Mr. Pill's Pet Pill Bug

Also by Victoria A. Berry

PUTTING THE DAZZLE BACK IN YOUR RAZZLE

Mr. Pill's Pet Pill Bug

A story for children of all ages.

by

Victoria A. Berry

Mr. Pill's Pet Pill Bug

A story for children of all ages.

Copyright © by Victoria A. Berry

ISBN: 9798699962686

The typist is indebted to her sweetness,
Mr. Pill, for gifting her this story.

INTRODUCTION

This is Mr. Pill's story, as told to his human, Binky. Every word of it is true.

CHAPTER ONE ~ MEET MR. PILL

One rainy day, Mr. Pill burst through the cat flap, stood on the area rug in the little home office, legs spread apart like a Sumo wrestler, and shook the water off himself.

Sumo wrestler pose.

Droplets flew everywhere. They sprinkled onto Binky, the human into whose house he and his four siblings had been born many Springs earlier. From the beginning, Mr. Pill has had a weakness for Binky and a great fondness for this place, a cozy cottage by the sea.

No one was surprised when Mr. Pill, his parents, siblings, and extended family of aunts and uncles, had each decided, on his or her own, to keep the human and to make this cottage their home. And why not? There was always someone to play with; a bunch of wild and wondrous places to explore; fun, colorful and interesting neighbors; several sun-splashed windowsills upon which to catch an afternoon nap; and enough room on Binky's bed so they could all huddle up in a warm bundle during the long Winter nights.

There was continuous support, safety in numbers, and comfort in togetherness. And, oh yes, oodles and oodles of love.

These days, it is just Mr. Pill and Binky who reside in the little bungalow on the bay. Because, sadly, one by one, their other family members have gone away. But, happily, over the last several Springs that they've been alone, Mr. Pill and Binky have been growing closer and closer. They've been bonding more tightly together, trying to plug the holes in each other's souls.

In that staunchly determined way of his, Mr. Pill keeps perfecting how to make his human's heart swell. With equal resolve, Binky continues learning how to fill her sweet boy to the brim with unbridled affection.

Even so, both missed their family and friends. Although they knew better, they ached for that love they felt had left them when they lost their dear ones.

Before entering the home office on this rainy day, Mr. Pill had stood outside that miniature backdoor of his, peering through the flap's clear plastic.

Oh no.

Binky's shoulders were slumped, her head was bent, and she seemed to be shaking a little. Pill worried that his human might be leaking water out of her eyes. This happened periodically. But Pill knew that exploding into Binky's office drenching wet would, strangely enough, dry her eyes, then make them light up. It succeeded 99% of the time.

That's why, seconds earlier, he had performed this trick.

Sure enough, his sudden eruption into the room worked its magic. Binky swiveled in the chair and burst out laughing at the sight of her frazzley drazzley sweet pea.

She jumped up, swiping the water off her cheeks with the back of a hand. And, in so doing, she brushed away the reason why they were wet in the first place. She'd been getting more and more worried about where her adored pet had gone. Binky had been calling and calling for him, but Mr. Pill had not returned. For the last two hours, Binky's stomach had been tied in knots. She'd been sick with dread that something awful had happened. But now here he was, her silly, mischievous boy. Finally! All was well once more.

Binky was so relieved that Pill was back home, safe and sound, that she wanted to gather the light of her life up in her arms and cover him with kisses. But first things first; sopping up his soaking wet fur. She held one arm out straight while telling the big, soggy mess,

"Stay right there. Don't move a muscle."

He did stay. And he did not move, not one single muscle.

Mr. Pill knew that this Sumo wrestler stance of his was an ideal visual image of just how phenomenal a feline he truly was. No doubt about it; *he* was the perfect embodiment of the most self-assured animal you could ever meet. When he'd stand like this, looking for all the world like master of the universe, Binky wished she could bottle up that bravado and gift it to anyone who needed a bolstering boost of self-confidence.

Binky tried not to laugh too much at the sight. Being long-haired, Pill carried half the yard in with him. Twigs, pine needles, leaves, rose petals, tiny pebbles, bits of bark, sand, and a bunch of other stuff all seemed to gravitate to him where, usually, they'd be held in place by spider webs. The boy was so dauntless, however, that he never seemed to notice that wearing the outdoors like an overcoat marred the Picture of Pussy Cat Perfection. He had no idea how funny he actually looked.

Nevertheless, to be on the safe side, Binky quickly turned away, holding a hand over her mouth.

She stepped into the laundry room to grab a clean towel off the top of the dryer. A stack was kept there precisely for these occasions. Before Mr. Pill could shake himself silly (or, more accurately, sillier), Binky gave the fuzzy headed stud muffin a thorough rub down. Mr. Pill liked this particular form of attention so much, he soon began squirming, as was his habit, so he could rush outside and crash back in again to repeat the process.

Binky, however, was not in favor of this plan. She was in her office because, well, she'd been working. Strike that; she had been *trying* to work. But, honestly, wouldn't you find it difficult to concentrate if your mind was preoccupied with the health and welfare of your best buddy? How could anyone hope to accomplish anything when one's sweetie pie was out in a storm, not hearing his loved one's calls, unaware he should return home?

You do see, don't you? Yes. You, too, would find it impossible to work under those circumstances.

Under normal conditions, when the human was, in fact, actually working and not busy wringing her hands, she required the use of electronic things. In order to function, electrical things like laptops, printers, chargers, desk lamps, smartphones and power strips all had to be plugged in and powered up.

Unbeknownst to this human, the long-haired black cat had a secondary purpose attached to the 'burst-through-the-cat-flap' routine. In addition to lighting up Binky's eyes and making her giggle, Pill hoped to help with the weekly housekeeping chores. Being one to clean himself after every meal and snack, as well as before each nap, Mr. Pill figured that the human's office items required a thorough washing down too.

The cat was of the opinion that, on occasion, the hard but warm, black or silver, blinking and glowing things in the office ought to be cleaned, if not by way of a rough tongue-licking, then, at a minimum, by way of a zealous cat's-shake-of-a-shower.

This may come as no revelation, but Binky was not of the same opinion. No, she was not.

She did not want Mr. Pill going outside, getting wet (and muddy) all over again, just to come back in to give the office equipment a shower. The human had no interest in electrocuting the electronics, not without a fair trial, in any event. And so, with one hand, she tried to keep the boy bundled up in the towel while, with her other hand, she tried to slide close the cat flap's lock.

Neither effort was working. Pill bounded out of the towel.

Just when she was reaching for her fuzzy-haired boy, which was just milliseconds after he had started his second big shake, both human and cat simultaneously stopped.

Just like that, they just stopped.

Together, the two watched as the smallest cannonball ever imagined got launched from somewhere inside Mr. Pill's long, black fur and took flight across the area rug.

"Me-wow."

It landed on the laminate floor, then went sliding into a file cabinet.

'Dink.'

It ricocheted back and bumped up against the rug where it came to a stop.

In unison, Binky and Pill turned toward one another. Her jaw dropped and his eyes widened.

Binky collapsed onto the cushy carpet. She and Mr. Pill crept to the edge of the rug, then each sat down; he, on his hind legs, and she, cross-legged.

For a while, the tiny cannonball just sat there. It did not fly. It did not crawl. It did not roll. It did not move, not at all. (Try as I might, it is just no use; I cannot unhear dear Dr. Seuss).

Mr. Pill turned to face Binky, then raised one eyebrow. Binky shrugged. The fuzz head blinked.

They returned their attention to the small ball on the ground in front of them. A full minute passed.

Finally, something started happening. Pill and Binky leaned forward.

CHAPTER TWO ~ MR. PILL MEETS A PILL BUG

The tiny cannonball unfurled, revealing itself to be a pill bug.

It took a few seconds to right itself. Bear in mind, after coming out of a ball, pill bugs have to turn themselves downside up from upside down. And then they have to get all of their itty-bitty feet set down in all the right places.

While the little guy rolled one way, then the other, flipped this way, then flopped that way, Binky and Mr. Pill held their breaths.

"Ta da!" exclaimed the former cannonball, having succeeded in straightening himself out with all of his feet on the floor right where they should be.

"Howl-lo," the cat gushed in greeting.

In order to get a good look at the new arrival, Pill leaned so far forward that Binky thought he would tip over.

Although cats are rather good at keeping their balance, they are a little less so when overcome with curiosity.

And Mr. Pill was most certainly overcome with curiosity.

He sat back. With rapt attention, Pill's eyes stayed glued to the pill bug as the tiny insect shifted his weight to his back legs and lifted his front end off the floor. The little bug with a helmet for a head began swaying back and forth, waving hello.

Itty bitty pill bug, by the edge of the rug.

These are the kinds of hellos that require using most of one's body. Dogs are experts at these, tail-wagging so vigorously (like, when their mistresses come home), that their entire bodies are involved in the wiggle-wag-wave.

When Mr. Pill came in closer for another good look, he saw that the pill bug's sway began at the bottom and continued up the length of its body until it reached its antennae on the top of its head. Each protrusion from the little guy's helmet twitched a few times, which the cat, quite understandably (and correctly), took to be a wave 'hello.'

Pill's chest started to pitter-pat.

'What a dude!' thought Pill. He sighed. And instantly recognized the sound. It sounded like those soft, cooing purrs Binky makes when she's looking at him with those ga ga eyes.

Insatiable curiosity shook the cat out of his little trance. Mr. Pill asked his first question,

"Dude! How did you *do* that?"

The pill bug thought about it and shook his tiny head. His antennae shook too.

See it now?

Pill contemplated things for a while, then crumpled onto the rug and curled up into as tight of a ball as he could. Binky assumed Pill was ready to take a nap, so she got up, sat down at her desk and went back to work. For real. Bo---ring.

From somewhere under all the fur and paws, Mr. Pill garbled, "Do I look like you did?"

The pill bug's antennae jiggled.

Mr. Pill heard a teeny tiny little voice shyly reply, "I don't know. Maybe. From down here, I can only see the top of your head."

"Oh." Pill uncurled himself, raised his head and, unable to contain his curiosity, asked his next question.

"How come you don't land on your paws?"

The pill bug lifted up a bit, then hunched down. If he had been born with shoulders, that movement would have been a shrug. Anyway, that's how Pill interpreted it.

"You have so many paws, that, surely, shouldn't half get turned around to set you upright by the time you reach the ground?" Pill's curiosity persisted.

"You'd think." In a louder, less shy voice, the bug said, "That's one thing I've been trying to learn. But even though I work on it every day, I still haven't been able to convert from all balled up, to all feet on the ground, in one simple, quick twist. But I'll keep practicing."

"Good on you!" Pill exclaimed. "I bet if you do, then surely someday soon you'll have it down pat."

"Stop calling me Shirley."

"Huh?"

"As well as Pat."

"Pat?"

"Just now you called me Pat."

"I did?"

"Before that, you called me Shirley. Twice."

The pill bug straightened himself to his full height, looked Pill in the eye and told him, "To be clear, my name is Sherman. It is not Shirley. Not Pat."

The big cat sat there, scrunched his face, blinked a few times to clear his head, wondering what was going on. How did he goof up?

Just then, the little bug flashed Pill a big smile. Pill's face instantly smoothed itself out and his eyes sparkled with relief. He gave the bug a big smile in return.

The bug brought his top right hands to his helmet head in a salute, then solemnly stated, "I, sir, am Sergeant First Class Sherman Tank the eight thousand, eight hundred and eighty-eighth."

The cat, mimicking the bug, put on his serious face and stood at attention.

CHAPTER THREE ~ GETTING TO KNOW ONE ANOTHER

"But you can call me Sherman." Beaming at the cat, the pill bug tipped gracefully over onto his side, thrust out all his arms and legs, wiggled them and said, "Glad to meet ya."

Grinning, Pill splayed his left paw and inched it towards Sherman, saying, "Likewise, I'm sure, Sergeant, er… Sherman Tank, the 8888th."

Not the least bit undereducated, having been on Binky's lap when she's reading and when she's watching moving pictures and listening to sounds which come out of a big rectangle in the den, Pill was, in fact, familiar with tanks. But, he thought, those in the picture books and on the lighted, noisy screen seemed a lot bigger and more angular than the short dude on the floor.

The US Army's Sherman tank

On the other paw, Sherman was an armored vehicle, of sorts, wasn't he? mused the cat.

With these facts in mind, Mr. Pill told his new buddy, "That's a great name! And, very appropriate, if I may say."

"You may and thank you!" Sherman replied. "What is your name?"

"Pill."

Each of Sherman Tank's antenna formed question marks.

The cat realized that further explanation was necessary. "My birth certificate says, 'Mr. Pill S. Berry.'"

Clear as mud. The antennae twisted together into a knot.

Pill hadn't noticed. He was too busy shining up his right forepaw's claws on his magnificent mane.

Eventually, Pill looked at Sherman for the anticipated response, the usual groveling or face full of wonderment. But Pill's new acquaintance exhibited no such display that one would normally expect from a being who was in the presence of WOW. Somewhat puzzled, but only momentarily, Pill heaved his impressive chest and exhaled a significant sigh. Waiting a theatrical five seconds for effect, the cat continued,

"Here I am." Pill sat up straighter, turned about 15 degrees to his left to better show off his noble profile, then pointed his nose up to the ceiling. The roly poly watched but did not say anything.

"I have entered the building." Pill glanced down at the little bug, cleared his throat, lifted his chin, and informed the newcomer, who, quite obviously was unclear on the subject, "You can applaud now."

Sherman slowly began clapping half-heartedly, using his right hands only, then wondered why and stopped.

"Have you no idea that you are in the presence of, of...um...what does Binky call it? Oh yes, a force to be reckoned with?"

"Oh that, I have no doubt," agreed Sherman. "But I'm not sure that explains why your name is Pillsberry."

"The human says I can be a real pain in the pituty, a pill."

The antennae disentangled themselves. "Ah ha," said Sherman, "Pill! Yes, I see. Because you're always getting into trouble."

"Frankly, I don't see it, that pain in the pituty part. The force to be reckoned with? Oh yeah. But I can't help it if trouble comes to me, now, can I? I don't go looking for problems; they come looking for me. One minute I'm doing my thing, being me, and the next minute, I'm somehow in a pickle, ya know?"

Sherman nodded. Both antennae bobbled as if on broken mattress springs.

Mr. Pill stole a side long glance at Binky, who appeared to be busy watching the lighted screen which, presently, was filled with playing cards moving around on a green background. He turned back to Sherman and leaned down.

"You should know something about me," Pill told the pill bug conspiratorially. "Take this as fair warning: me and Calliope Curiosity have a thing going on. She comes calling for me day in, day out. Her voice is so beautiful, that I can't help but follow her wherever she goes. I've had such a crush on Calliope," Pill whispered, "that, because of her, I'm almost always getting tossed off, or thrown out, of things."

The itty-bitty blank face stared up at Pill. Despite having met less than ten minutes earlier, Sherman had already surmised that this cat's middle name should be 'Trouble,' with a capital T.

"Seriously." Pill told him.

'Tell me something I don't know,' the perplexed bug was thinking, but to his credit, kept his mouth shut.

The alert cat scanned the little office, just in case someone was listening in or spying on them.

Greek muse, Calliope, in a painting by Simon Vouet.

"No matter what kind of trouble Calliope Curiosity leads me into," the cat continued, his green irises glittering, "I always end up on my paws." Mr. Pill nodded at the pill bug. "Whatever I land on, it never hurts too much because my pads are big, squishy cushions."

Proud of his many and varied attributes, Pill extended a forearm out over the edge of the rug, and being careful not to scare or touch Sherman, he splayed his furry toes apart.

The little pill bug bobbed his helmet head up and down appreciatively.

Not to be outdone, however, Sherman told Mr. Pill, "Well, I've got armored plates! See?" The pill bug scooted his butt around to show off his half dozen hard plates. They were each curved, like wide belts that encircled only the back of his body and seemed to slide independently of the other plates. The six segments were stacked one on top of the other, running from his helmet head down to his bottom.

"Me-wow!"

"I'm built Tank-tough. Me and my ancestors, we've always had to take on anything the enemy can throw at us. Nothing sticks. And usually, nothing hurts. Being a roly poly, I can quickly take cover, deploy instantly and keep on the move with these interior inline tracked limbs and exterior sliding plates. You might say that Sergeant First Class Sherman Tank, the 8888th is an expert at rolling with the punches, yes siree."

Sherman shadow boxed with his top six arms.

"Pow, pow! Jab, jab!"

Pill was fascinated by the puny pugilist.

Sherman said, "All these armored plates? They cover the entire back side of me, so they keep me protected while I cruise the demilitarized zone and check in with my troops. All this?"

Sherman twisted in the opposite direction. His numerous armored plates glinted in the light of Binky's desk lamp. "This is how I roll, uh huh, yes sir. And when I encounter danger, I go into a curl and take cover inside where I will stay safe and sound."

'Safe and sound,' Pill repeated to himself.

Both thought their own thoughts for a few seconds.

"Binky keeps me safe and sound. That's the main reason why I try so hard to ignore Calliope Curiosity. You believe me, don't you Sherman?"

Before Sherman knew what he was doing, he started nodding his head up and down.

"Honestly. I really do try to stay out of trouble, because, this is what I figure; if Binky's happy, then I'm happy. Catch my drift?"

He couldn't help it; the roll-with-the-punches roly poly was nodding nonstop.

"That's why," Pill continued, "many Springs ago, I became a cat that goes with the flow, ya know?"

Sherman snapped out of his monotonous head nodding.

"Speaking of the flow," the pill bug piped up, "I was flowing down a river next to the third root from the left of the smooth, black beach stone in the moss under the Monterey pine out there when you laid down. I guess you didn't see me, but, when you got up again, you picked me up."

"Oh my gosh, I didn't hurt you, did I?" asked Pill anxiously.

"Heck no. I am Sergeant First Class Sherman Tank, the 8888th. As such, I am prepared for anything with any number of contingency plans."

"You tucked and rolled yourself into a ball."

"My primary, first choice, go-to plan, yes."

"How many other plans are there?"

"Hmm, let's see." Sherman held out a few arms, started to count, then dropped them. "OK, so I only have the one plan, but it works for..."

"...for everything. I agree, why reinvent the wheel?"

"Exactly. And, having just the one plan, I've got that down to an 'O.'"

"You mean a 'T'?

"No, an 'O,' for the shape. Os are round and turn. Ts are not, so don't. I'm Sergeant First Class Sherman Tank, the 8888th, an *Armadillidiidae* and that, sir, is why I roll."

"How you roll."

"That too."

The little dude paused. Decided, even if it hurt to completely unfurl, to expose his vulnerable side, so to speak, he just had to go ahead and lay himself out there.

With that decision made, Sherman said, "Seen as how we're baring our souls, there's something you don't know about me which you should know."

"If you're talkin' about earlier, claiming I picked you up, you think I didn't know?"

"Umm...didn't know what?"

"That you've got a thing for me." The cat closed his eyes and sang, "And you can't let go."

Sherman was dazed. He'd had no idea what to expect from the cat after trying to disclose his predicament, but it certainly wasn't this.

"Huh?" (Not exactly the pill bug's most insightful, nor most brilliantly conceived question, but on short notice, it'd have to do).

"Just like Calliope Curiosity does, you've been following me. I'm right, aren't I?"

Sherman's jaw dropped. Eventually he stammered, "Oh, gee...that isn't what I was going to say, but...Hey, wait a sec. So, you knew that that was *not* the first time you've carried me somewhere?"

Pill nodded. "You'd be amazed if you knew what I know. And, what I know, little dude, is that I am prac-ti-cat-ly im-paws-ible to resist. Today was not your first time."

"Not by a long shot. I've been hitching rides with you, flumping up and off you for a long, long time."

Huh? Now Pill was taken aback.

"You're not a member of my fan club? Don't want my paw print? Not hounding me for a photo?"

Sherman shook his helmet head back and forth.

"Then, why?"

"Like I said, flumping. That's a combination of flinging and jumping. See, I'm trying to flump myself up as high as I can get. And, maybe someday, I'll reach my target."

"Which is?" Pill asked, forgetting he might be enticing Calliope to come out and play.

"The moon."

"The moon?! Sherman, why do you want to go there?" The cat checked the office doors, windows and the cat flap. Whew! No sign of Ms. Curiosity. Not yet.

"Because the moon is close to heaven. That's where the stars live. And lots of those stars are my relations. I've never met half of them. As for the others, I haven't seen them in many, many Springs. But I want to visit because, well it's like this, I miss them."

Sherman looked up at the ceiling. Nothing there but a low, flat, white surface. He closed his tiny eyes and imagined the night sky.

Mr. Pill glanced up too. "Your relatives are stars?" Boy, if he only knew just how close Calliope was.

"Yes, sir!"

The cat's jaw dropped.

"That's why I have made it my mission in lives to go there."

Before Sherman could say more, Pill interrupted. "Did you say 'lives'? More than one?"

"Yes, sir, I did."

"You too? Same here! Wow!" The cat scratched an ear. "And in this life, the one you're livin' now, you aim to go way up there to visit former pill bugs who are now stars?"

Sherman inclined his helmet head forward reverently.

"That is way cool," Pill told him. "So you were saying? About this life's mission?"

"It's to go to the moon. And I'm going to use any method I can muster to get me there. That's why I flump onto you. Because, maybe where you're going is a place where I can flump higher. And from there, get somewhere higher still, until I can hitch a ride onto a shooting star, and while it's going by the moon, I'll flump myself onto it."

The little dude took a deep breath, then exhaled. "That's my dream anyways. Probably sounds stupid to you." Under his helmet, Sherman peeked up at Pill.

"No! Are you kidding? No way! What a lofty goal, dude. Gee, you have relatives in the night sky? Me-wow! I don't think I've ever met anybody who has actual, real stars for relatives!"

"Well, they are *distant* relatives."

"Still, stars nevertheless. Gosh..."

If pill bugs gloated, Sherman would be gloating. Big time. But they don't. Despite Sherman's hidden desire to gloat, being neither the self-centered nor selfish type, he found he was unable to keep the reason for such a big gloat to himself. This piece of information was just too good to be kept a secret. And so, Sherman told Pill,

"You have relatives up there too."

"I do?!" The cat was incredulous.

"Yes sir, most definitely."

His razzler lit up; Pill had just been star-struck.

Zing - Bonk!

After a few dazzling thoughts collided inside his head, the cat realized that it hadn't hurt one bit. In fact, it had been astronomically uplifting.

Sherman smiled. He was glad he told Pill about this and elucidated on the subject, "Everybody does. You know why? Because we're all descendants of the Big Bright Stars."

"I've got stars in my family? Up there?" Pill hopped up and went over to the tall office window and looked outside. It was almost completely dark, but cloudy and raining. He couldn't see a single relative. Maybe tomorrow night. He went back over to Sherman and asked,

"So, you wanna go visit your relatives and ..."

"*Our* relatives," Sherman corrected. "Mine, yours, everyone's." Sherman turned around to look at Binky.

"Everyone's?" Pill asked, gazing up at his human. "Even Binky's?"

Sherman nodded.

"And you want my help?"

Holding Pill's eyes, Sherman nodded again.

"But why use *me* to do your flumping? I mean, why'd you pick me when you could have hitched a ride with Kiki, the Blue Jay? He flies for a living. Or the Monarchs? When they're in town I bet they'd help get you to the top of the Monterey pine."

"Hmmm...Why did I choose you, Mr. Pill?"

Sherman Tank, the 8888th, curled himself into his own rocking chair, leaned back and rocked.

"Well sir, originally, I selected you because you're the softest, fluffiest pillow I've ever found, whether I am flumping or not."

Mr. Pill puffed up. He couldn't help it. Next, he started preening. Again, because he couldn't help it.

While rocking and watching the cat primp, Sherman continued,

"And I soon discovered that you're way more than a big, soft pillow. You're a nice guy. Always careful with me. You haven't got a sharp pincer, obnoxious stink gland, nasty sting, bristly or sticky coating, nor a repellent plate of armor on you."

The cat, who'd had a rear paw in the air, tweezing a burr out with his front fangs, tipped over backwards, then rolled, like he'd meant to do that. Sherman carried on, acting as if he hadn't noticed Pill's *faux* paw.

"Ever since my first flump onto you, I knew I could trust you. So, whenever I can, I try to ride with you. Because I know that I can flump onto you without worrying whether or not you'll safely catch, hold, then release me."

The little soldier gulped back a sob, then stole a quick glance at the cat. "It's *you* I want to be there for me when I do this. It's *you* I aim for when I jump. And until I accomplish my mission, it's you I want there while I'm practicing."

Pill stood and took on his Sumo wrestler pose. Holding his tail way up high, he began strutting. He strut his stuff in a circle going clockwise, then strut himself in a circle going counterclockwise. Mr. Pill S. Berry was so overcome with pride that he could barely contain himself.

'Me,' the cat thought to himself, 'He picked ***me***!'

Pill's heart fluttered. Never in his life had anybody other than Binky made him feel so a-twitter-pated.

CHAPTER FOUR ~ MR. PILL POPS THE QUESTION

And, wouldn't you know it, dear reader, but this was the exact moment when Mr. Pill decided to adopt Sergeant First Class Sherman Tank, the 8888th. He was so enamored with this *Armadillidiidae* that Pill wanted the pill bug to be his very own pet. It never occurred to full of chutz-paw Pill S. Berry, who'd rarely in his life taken 'no' for an answer, that the tiny dude might not be OK with that.

Suddenly, Sherman blasted out of his rocking position, grabbed his face with several hands and cried, "Sir! You get me so discombobulated that I keep forgetting to tell you that really, and I mean *really*, important thing that you must know about me."

"I'm sure that whatever it is won't change my opinion, nor my intentions. I know all I need to know about you, Sherman."

"Your intentions? Look, you need to listen to me. I've got myself into a jam. It's what us Tank Family members call a SNAFU. I know I'm the one who deliberately flumped onto you, and it's not your fault that you left the Monterey pine and came in here. Um…and…"

The pill bug nervously wrung his many hands. He had to tell the cat that super important thing. Right now. He had to spit it out even though he couldn't make spit. With a parched palate he forged on, "And, well, I know I told you that I roll with the punches, I'm tough and can handle whatever is thrown my way but, well it's like this: I don't see any rivers in here."

Pill turned left, then turned right, verifying, nope, no rivers in Binky's office.

"And it doesn't appear to be raining."

Pill looked up at the ceiling, then stuck a paw out. No raindrops as far as he could tell.

"In other words, um...there's no water around."

"Not here. For some reason, Binky doesn't like what happens when water comes into contact with..." Pill eyed the plugged-in items blinking and glowing around Binky's desk.

Sherman followed Pill's gaze. "No of course not!" The tiny bug laughed one of those fakey kind of 'put on a brave face' laughs. His antennae twitched. Sherman looked down, then back up at Pill and said, "I, myself, don't mind getting wet. Because, like I said, that's how I roll. Good old roly poly me. Rolling with the punches..."

Pill kept looking at where he thought the little dude's itty-bitty eyes should be, somewhere under that helmet he was wearing.

The helmet head mumbled, "Rolling and flumping, away from home and all its comforts. Away to a place I don't know, that hasn't got those, er, basic necessities and now here I am."

Pill sat back and exclaimed, "Yes! Here you are indeed! And I am so glad!"

An odd but not unwelcome, warm, tingly feeling, one he'd never had before, whooshed over Sherman Tank. He felt charged up, like he was a buzzing firefly. The heat parched his throat. He was thirstier than ever. Yes sir, he could sure use some water right about now.

Pill carried on, "I'm so glad you're here because I really like you and..."

"What?!" Did Sherman hear right? "You *like* me? You? Like *me*? Oh sir, I like you too!"

"You do?! That is super cool, dude!", Pill purred.

Although Sherman was thrilled to pieces, he was getting more and more nervous. He had to tell Pill that really important thing. But just when he was about to unload, the cat spoke again,

"So, Sherman, can I ask you something? Oh gosh, I hope you say 'yes.'"

Putting his urgent need aside, as any good battle-ready comrade would, Sherman Tank came to attention and addressed the cat as if Pill was his drill sergeant, "Sir, yes sir! Ask me anything. Go ahead, shoot."

"OK. Well, what I want to ask is, oh boy, you're gonna think this is coming out of left field, but I gotta know, ya know? I can't just not ask, cuz then I'd never know and then what?"

"Please, carry on." Sherman was becoming more frantic by the moment. He tapped a few impatient toes. "Fire away!"

"Alright, here goes. I think you're super and want to hang out with you. Anywhere and anytime we can. It'd be easy to do that if you were, umm, if you could be my pet. Ya know?"

Now, friendly reader, you know and I know what Sherman's answer will be. Of course he'll agree to take on whatever assignment Pill might ask of him. What creature in his right mind would not be OK with that? This was especially true of a flumping pill bug named Sergeant First Class Sherman Tank, the 8888th.

But, as you've likely discerned, there's a slight problem. Maybe not a big one, but a bit of a dilemma, nonetheless.

Sherman had no idea what a pet was.

So he asked Pill.

"Righteous question, dude. Let me think."

Sherman hoped this wouldn't take long. Much as he needed to know what a pet was, much as he really liked Pill and wanted to assist him however he could, he really had to ...

"I'm not really sure either except I know I am one. That's what Binky tells other humans, that I am her pet," Pill said thoughtfully.

Sherman's patience was getting put to the test, stuck inside on this rainy afternoon.

"Oh, man... She gives me such a good feeling about myself..." Pill sighed, and sat there, staring off into space. And looking to Sherman like he was mentally absent without leave.

Sherman counted the seconds as they ticked by. Hooah – oorah – hooyah! Man was he getting lots of training in this waiting business.

'...six, seven, eight...' Sherman counted to himself.

"Everyone should feel that good about themselves, don't you agree?" Pill pondered.

The question acted like a bugle call at sunrise for the little warrior. Sherman came instantly alert. Although he'd never considered this question, he realized he agreed. Why shouldn't everyone feel good about themselves? Now he was impatient to learn more.

Pill, off in la la land, roused himself. "Being someone's pet is the most marvelous thing, Sherman. I can hardly put into words how special Binky makes me feel." The cat pawsed. "As far as she's concerned, I can do no wrong. She loves me no matter what. Ya know?"

Poor Sherman did not know, not personally. The brave soldier tried to maintain a strong facade. But it was difficult because Pill was piercing the *Armadillidiidae*'s armor with his description of what it was like to be Binky's pet.

And that's why he almost missed what Pill was saying. When the little bug's antennae finally tuned back in, he wasn't sure he'd heard right.

"What?" stuttered shell-shocked Sherman.

"I said, now that you know what a pet is, what do you think? Will you be my mine?"

"Ya, ya, ya your pet?" the little guy stuttered.

"Please? I know I'm not describing it very well, but trust me, it's a good thing. Because, gosh Sherman, every time Binky sees me, she gets this goofy grin, her eyes light up and her heart springs open and I feel like I'm her birthday present, all wrapped in pretty paper and tied up in a bow."

Sherman nodded. It was all he could do not to cry.

Pill gazed fondly at Binky. Sherman scootched around to look at the human. Right then, kid you not, the human turned their way. And smiled.

"Hello my sweetness. My light. Are you getting hungry? How 'bout I feed you when I finish this stupid game?"

The cat's eyes softened. Then blinked. Pill shifted his attention back to Sherman.

"When you're a pet, that means you're adored. And protected. You feel safe and sound, like what you said happens when you curl up into your ball."

"Safe and sound," murmured the pill bug.

"You're in that zone, dude, where no matter what happens, you'll always end up landing on your paws. To be loved unconditionally gives you the strength to deal with anything. It also gives you the complete freedom to simply be yourself." Pill sighed. "It's an awesome thing realizing someone loves and cares about you that much."

Sherman's eyes came out of hiding from under the helmet, two bright spots shimmering like itsy bitsy pools reflecting moonlight. Both were quiet. The only sound came from the computer, cards shuffling and being dealt. Binky was losing another game of Solitaire.

"Cherish is the word that keeps coming to mind," said Pill. "Being Binky's pet has made me realize that I want to cherish someone like she does me. You know how you told me your dream? I'll tell you mine. It's to make someone feel as good about himself as Binky makes me feel."

Sherman blew his nose on one set of hands. Pill could hear the honk a foot away.

"And, since you told me a secret, Sherman, I'll tell you one: love is everlasting. Like you, I've had many lives. This is like my fourth or fifth. But it wasn't until this one that I found that I could believe it myself, so don't waste any time wondering if we remain connected with one another. We do. Our love for one another goes on forever and ever."

The pill bug and Pill looked at one another for a long time. It was as if Pill was passing this truth to Sherman via direct eye contact while Sherman was verifying Pill's statement by way of how the refractions of green and gold lights danced in the cat's eyes.

"If all my dreams come true, I'll be spending time with you." Pill hummed a few bars. Still holding Sherman's eyes, Pill rephrased the question, "So do we have a deal little buddy?"

"Huh?" Another 'zing – bonk' moment. This time Sherman's razzler lit up.

"Whadda you say?" the normally impatient cat asked with the utmost patience.

The short dude grew twice his regular height. Sherman's chest visibly thump thumped. He began dancing a jig, which was no easy task when one has so many legs.

"Good." Pill's whiskers curved into a smile. "First order of business is to get you back outside where it's wet, or you're going to wither up, turn to powder and blow away."

Sherman stopped dancing. He was so astounded, so relieved, that he toppled over.

"Oh, thank you! How did you know? I didn't think…Good golly I thought I was a goner." He dropped his head onto the floor and took a few big breaths. "Pill bugs are different. We need more water than most critters. Lots more than most bugs. I guess we're flawed."

"Flawed? Huh? Dude!"

"Yes sir, me especially. I try to hide it because soldiers are supposed to soldier on, even without water. But I can't."

"Who could?"

"Almost all the other Tank family members. I'm sure I'm a disappointment to everyone. You'd be better off if you just gave me my marching orders so I can be on my way."

"On your way? Oh, Sherman I'd be worse off, all of us would if you went away. What ridiculous nonsense… You, a disappointment? Flawed? Honestly!" Pill shook his head. "I may not know much yet, but this I do know: it's what's inside us that matters. Our cores. Yours? Dude. The brightness of your spirit, that dogged courage of yours, and the way your heart gleams with goodness. Those are the first things that got me, Sherman. I can see your true self shine even through all that armor of yours. To me, you blaze more brilliantly than one of the Big Bright Stars."

Once again, Pill peered at the place just under Sherman's helmet, hoping to lock eyes with the little dude. The roly-poly lifted his head. There they were, Sherman's eyes, twinkling back at him.

"I should've known your relatives are stars cuz you are one amazingly dazzling dude!"

"I am?"

Pill purred an avalanche of yeses, nearly rolling Sherman over.

"I'm sorry that I was messin' with ya like that, pretending I didn't know how much hydration an *Armadillidiidae* needs. You gotta remember I'm new at having a pet. You're my very first," Pill said.

Before they both collapsed into shapeless mounds of mortified mush, the cat carried on,

"Take note, Sherman; as pets, we learn that we're gonna get teased. And expected to play crazy games. And we'll hear them talking to us in baby voices, calling us funny names."

"Like sweetness?" asked Sherman.

"Well, that one is all right, but 'little baby boy,' makes me cringe sometimes. Actually, not so much anymore. Because the way Binky says it, it comes out sounding like fresh cream pouring into your bowl."

Pill's stomach growled. "Another thing, Sherman - on occasion, you probably should come when you're called, so keep an ear out. It's usually because it's dinner time. Lastly, aw sheesh, I almost hate to say this, but... be prepared to get covered in kisses."

Pill shot Sherman a big smile. The little guy raised his eyes up at his antennae, which had twirled themselves into a big heart.

The Antennae Galaxies. When the two merged, they formed the shape of a heart. (Image from Hubblesite.org)

"All right, sweetness," Binky said, pushing her chair away from the desk. She was looking down behind her, making sure she was a good distance away from the pill bug. Mr. Pill seemed fascinated by the little guy. It appeared that her sweet pea had found a friend.

The cat told Sherman, "Binky gives me the ultimate in kitty-cat-contentment. I discovered in this life that she does these things because she likes hangin' with me. And it's her way of letting me know that I'm super wanted. That I am loved unconditionally." Pill sighed, then continued, "I promise, little buddy, that soon you will feel, way deep down right here," Pill thumped his chest with one paw, "an incredible, engulfing, unending, amazing love."

Sherman thumped his tiny chest too and nodded.

"You ready for a little din din, huh little baby boy?"

Pill's eyes automatically darted up to Binky's, then darted back to Sherman's.

"Ahhh," the human sighed. She got out of the chair and stepped carefully around the pill bug and Pill. She went over to the back door and put her hand on the knob.

Pill turned to look at Binky again; she raised an eyebrow, he nodded. Supremely satisfied, the cat murmured, "Synchronis-kitty."

Grinning, Binky opened the back door, and tip-toed past the two new buddies. She had gotten the message that Pill wanted to go outside before having dinner.

Pill told Sherman, "Same wavelength. Me and her. We read each other's thoughts. No doubt you and me will be…"

"… doing that eventually," they both said in unison.

Pill's ears and Sherman's antennae twitched uncontrollably like live wires.

Taking a swipe at the left side of his head, then another at the right side, Pill told Sherman, "How about this - tomorrow, you can practice flumping on me all day long. Sound good?"

The small soldier leapt. It was such a huge and enthusiastic leap, that he had to use most of his hands and feet to grab ahold of Pill's ear so as not to overshoot his mark.

Swinging from the right ear's hairs, Sherman cooed, "Mr. Pill, I think you're going to be as great at this having a pet business as your Binky is."

"Really? Dude! You're not just sayin' that?"

Sherman Tank gave an affectionate little tug on the long white hairs that grew from the center of Pill's ears.

The cat stood, then stretched. "Well, you know what I've heard?"

"What have you heard?"

"That it helps to have a great pet to begin with," Pill wrinkled his nose, "my sweetness."

Sherman let go of the ear hairs and slid down Pill's soft, sleek nose. While hugging it with all of his might, and with almost zero embarrassment, the newly minted pet gushed,

"Aw, sheesh…"

About the Typist

Shortly after Vicki (Binky) Berry's family of two humans and four adult cats moved to a small coastal town, a young female feline came to visit. She, in turn, was visited nightly by a suitor who would become Pill's father. After Pill and his siblings were born, their tiny house seemed to burst at the seams. A "free kittens" sign was posted. Appointments were made. When the first potential adopters arrived for a look, there wasn't a kitten in sight. The humans had hidden them away, unable to part with a single one.

Everything in this story is true. Mr. Pill really did grow up in a beach cottage along with his mom, dad, four siblings, aunts and uncles. And, he really did have a pet pill bug.

How could Binky have known that? The first part of the answer is sad: Three weeks shy of his 19th birthday, Pill S. Berry, the last of the ten cats, Binky's sweet pea, died in her arms. Reviewing photos of her boy in the following weeks, Binky came across the ones she took of Pill and Sherman in her office. That night, she cried herself to sleep.

But here's the happy part: While she slept, her boy's spirit came blazing in as if he'd been riding on a shooting star to tell her this story. Kid you not. The following day, within a span of a few hours, Binky typed up the boy's narrative.

Mr. Pill's Pet Pill Bug is proof that love crosses time and space. Until learning Pill's tale, Binky would have thought this im-paw-sible to believe. But then she got zing-bonked too.